j I CAN READ Disney
Scollon, Bill,
The big battle /
9780736481557

 **W9-DET-392**

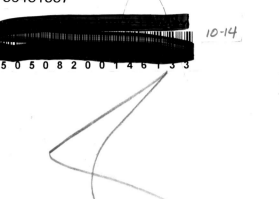

10-14

Dear Parents:

Congratulations! Your child is taking the first steps on an exciting journey. The destination? Independent reading!

STEP INTO READING® will help your child get there. The program offers five steps to reading success. Each step includes fun stories and colorful art or photographs. In addition to original fiction and books with favorite characters, there are Step into Reading Non-Fiction Readers, Phonics Readers and Boxed Sets, Sticker Readers, and Comic Readers—a complete literacy program with something to interest every child.

Learning to Read, Step by Step!

Ready to Read   **Preschool–Kindergarten**
• **big type and easy words** • **rhyme and rhythm** • **picture clues**
For children who know the alphabet and are eager to begin reading.

Reading with Help   **Preschool–Grade 1**
• **basic vocabulary** • **short sentences** • **simple stories**
For children who recognize familiar words and sound out new words with help.

Reading on Your Own   **Grades 1–3**
• **engaging characters** • **easy-to-follow plots** • **popular topics**
For children who are ready to read on their own.

Reading Paragraphs   **Grades 2–3**
• **challenging vocabulary** • **short paragraphs** • **exciting stories**
For newly independent readers who read simple sentences with confidence.

Ready for Chapters   **Grades 2–4**
• **chapters** • **longer paragraphs** • **full-color art**
For children who want to take the plunge into chapter books but still like colorful pictures.

STEP INTO READING® is designed to give every child a successful reading experience. The grade levels are only guides; children will progress through the steps at their own speed, developing confidence in their reading. Remember, a lifetime love of reading starts with a single step!

BATTLE CARDS!

Directions for two players:
Have a grown-up help you remove the battle cards from this book.

Shuffle the cards and divide them equally between both players.

Each player's deck should be facedown. Both players should show their top card at the same time, placing it faceup.

The player who puts down the card with the higher number value takes the cards and puts them in a "win" pile. If both cards have the same number value, each player puts down another card until someone has the higher number value.

When all the cards have been used, the player with more cards in their "win" pile is the winner.

Visit us on the Web!
StepIntoReading.com
randomhousekids.com

Educators and librarians, for a variety of teaching tools, visit us at RHTeachersLibrarians.com
ISBN 978-0-7364-3245-0 (trade) — ISBN 978-0-7364-8155-7 (lib. bdg.) — ISBN 978-0-7364-3246-7 (ebook)
Printed in the United States of America 10 9 8 7 6 5 4 3 2 1

Disney
BIG HERO 6

THE BIG BATTLE

By Bill Scollon

Illustrated by the Disney Storybook Art Team

Random House 🏠 New York

Meet Big Hero 6!
They are a team of friends
who always have fun together.
Sometimes they fight
bad guys!
Hiro is the leader.

Hiro is building an invention
for the Tech Showcase.
His friends want to help.

They meet at a junkyard
to search for spare parts.

Hiro is fourteen.

He is a robotics genius!

He has made cool new
inventions called microbots.
Hiro will bring his bots
to the Tech Showcase.

Baymax is a nurse bot,

a robot that can

scan a person

to check their health.

He is Hiro's friend.

Wasabi studies physics.
He likes finding new ways
to get organized.

Honey Lemon loves chemistry.

She is very good at it!

Honey makes mixtures

that do cool things.

Go Go Tomago knows about mechanics and engineering. Go Go likes to move fast!

Fred just likes
reading comic books
and hanging out.

At the Tech Showcase,
Hiro's microbots form a stage
for him to stand on.
His invention is a hit!
Hiro's friends are proud
of him.

There is a fire
at the showcase!
Someone set the fire
to steal the microbots.

Hiro leads the team
to find the villain
who stole his microbots.
The villain commands the
microbots to attack the team.

He chases their car.

They crash into the water!

Baymax rescues them.

Hiro and the
team plan to stop
the masked man.

They create high-tech gear from their inventions to fight the villain.

Wasabi gets amazing gloves with laser hands.
He practices slicing through everything in sight.

Honey gets a special purse.

Inside is a chemistry set

that makes all kinds

of super potions.

"I love it!" Honey says.

Go Go gets throwing discs
and wheels that give her
super speed.
"Cool!" she says
as she whizzes by.

Fred gets a fire-breathing
monster suit that can
super-jump.
"This is the best day of
my life!" he shouts.

Baymax gets body armor,
a rocket fist, powerful
thrusters, and wings!
Hiro and Baymax take
a test flight.

At first they fly low,
and then they fly high!
"Yeah!" cries Hiro.
They are off to
find the villain.

The team finds the villain.
They work hard to stop him.
The villain attacks each
member, one by one.

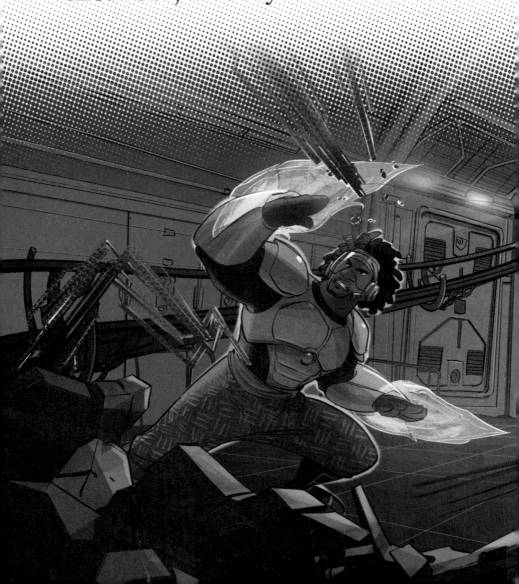

"Never quit!" Hiro shouts.
The microbots make the
villain hard to defeat.

The masked villain has built
a portal that could destroy
the city.

He commands the microbots
to attack Big Hero 6.
The team fights together.

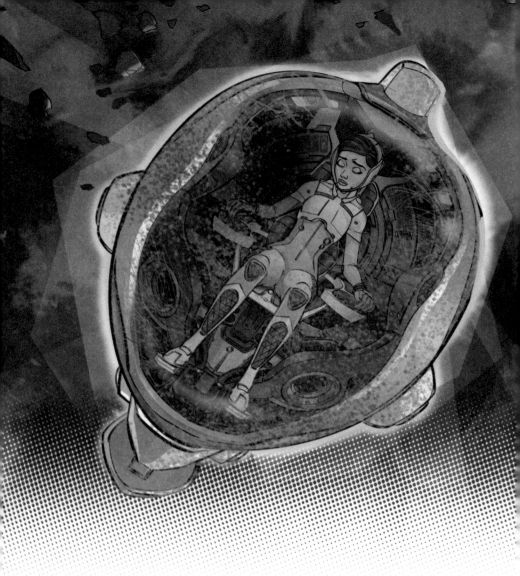

They defeat the villain.
Then they discover a girl
trapped in the portal!

Baymax and Hiro
work together.
They use Baymax's
rocket fist.
They save the girl!

The big battle is over!
Hooray for Big Hero 6!